The Invisible You

The Invisible You

by Alan Page and Kamie Page
artwork by David Geister

PAGE EDUCATION FOUNDATION
MINNEAPOLIS, MINNESOTA

Everything about Howard's new neighborhood was different. The streets were different. The houses were different. The yards were different.

The kids were different. And for the first time in his life, Howard felt like he was different—different from everything and everyone around him.

Howard stood in front of his new school. He held his mother's hand and offered a shaky smile to the faces staring back at him.

Howard had a habit of noticing people. He found one girl's freckles fascinating, and another's beaded braids hard to ignore. There was also a boy with greenish, catlike eyes. Howard almost forgot where he was and what he was doing. Almost.

As the kaleidoscope of kids captured Howard's attention, he lowered his eyes. He knew he wasn't supposed to stare. He knew he wasn't supposed to be noticing these things. He knew his parents never talked about people's differences, so he figured he shouldn't either.

Howard barely heard his mother ask, "You okay, bud?"

A quick "Mmm hmm" was all he could muster as he dragged his feet toward the door. He longed for his old school where everything had been normal—his classroom, his teachers, his friends, and himself.

Biting his lip, Howard entered the classroom. The teacher, Ms. Sims, smiled and led him to a table with three children he recognized from outside the school. The boy's name was Irving and the two girls were Bernie and Georgianna. The class was in the middle of independent reading, so Ms. Sims told Howard he should browse the classroom library for a book.

Before getting up, Howard couldn't help but sneak a peek at his new tablemates.

Irving's skin was a sandy buttermilk. He was busy reading a thick chapter book. His green eyes zipped past difficult words as his eyebrows raised and lowered with each sentence. Howard sighed. Irving's book looked much harder and more interesting than the easy chapter books he was used to reading. Howard just knew he wasn't going to fit in.

Bernie's skin was a freckly blend of soft caramel rye, and Georgianna's was a rich charcoal spice. The girls were too busy giggling and sharing a book to notice Howard as he tried to figure out what was so funny. He frowned. *They've probably been friends since kindergarten*, he thought. At that moment, he wondered what his old classmates were up to as an ache spread through his heart, filling him with dread.

Howard reluctantly chose a book from the shelf. He was only a few sentences in when Ms. Sims called the class to attention.

"Boys and girls, as you know, we have a new student starting today."

Howard shrunk as all eyes fell upon him.

"Could you come up, Howard, and share a few things about yourself so we can get to know you better?"

Oh, great, Howard thought as his hands began to sweat, his mouth dried out, and his knees started to shake. "Uhhh…"

Howard wasn't exactly sure where to begin.

His cheeks felt hot and his mind raced to think of something to say.

His silence was met with giggles that were stopped with a stern look from Ms. Sims.

"Sharing about yourself can be hard," she said. "Especially in front of people you don't know." She smiled at Howard. "I'm wondering if you could tell us a little bit about the invisible you."

Howard's face scrunched. "The what?"

"The invisible you," Ms. Sims encouraged.

"As you can see, each of us is unique. We have different skin colors, hair types, and eye shapes and shades. You've probably noticed differences in us, and we've noticed differences in you. Noticing is normal."

Howard's eyes shifted. No adult had ever spoken directly to him about people's differences or about what lived inside his heart. *Was it a trick? What kind of a teacher talks about this?*

Ms. Sims continued. "But these differences aren't what make us who we are. We also have an invisible part of

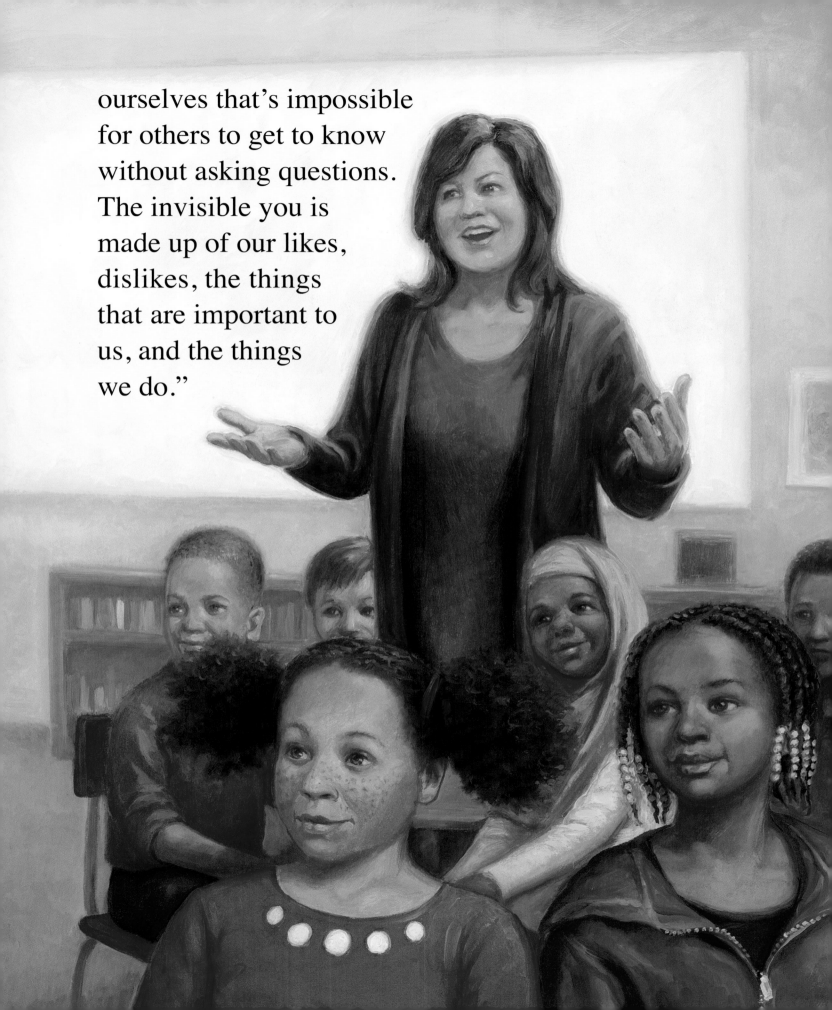

ourselves that's impossible for others to get to know without asking questions. The invisible you is made up of our likes, dislikes, the things that are important to us, and the things we do."

Howard looked down at his feet. "I'm not sure I…"

"I raise mealworms as pets and have the biggest insect collection on my block," interrupted Georgianna.

"I'm afraid of Georgie's insect collection," squeaked Irving.

Georgianna rolled her eyes.

"I'm serious!"

This time the giggles were muted, but Ms. Sims allowed the class to continue sharing.

"I live with my grandparents, who only speak Japanese," added Bernie.

Howard never would have guessed.

After several more students shared, Ms. Sims raised her eyebrows and gently looked at Howard.

Howard took a deep breath. He wasn't sure he knew what to say, but he also knew that he had to say something. At this point, anything was better than silence.

"Hmmm…" he wavered.

"Well…" he breathed.

"I like mysteries," he offered.

Irving's green eyes lit up as his fingers linked to show a connection had been made.

Howard continued, "And I used to play soccer on Saturdays in my old neighborhood at the park." He saw Bernie and Georgianna look at each other excitedly and smile.

"Thank you for sharing, Howard," Ms. Sims said. "We can't wait to learn more about you and share about the invisible us in the days ahead."

The rest of Howard's day raced by in a blur. He found out during writing time that Irving was writing a mystery and had decided to include Howard as a character.

At recess he discovered that Bernie and Georgianna were on a traveling soccer team, and they knew some of the same kids from Howard's old school.

On the walk home from school, Howard took a new look
at his new neighborhood. Sensing the spring in his step, his
mother asked, "So, how was your day?"

"It was great!" he said. "Mom, do you know you have an

Her eyebrows raised. "I do?"

Howard told his mother everything he had learned that day. He couldn't wait to go back to school and see his new friends. Everything was different. But as his teacher had said, differences are normal. And for Howard, normal is good.

PAGE EDUCATION
FOUNDATION

Creating Heroes Through Education & Service

The Page Education Foundation, started by Alan and Diane Page in 1988, assists Minnesota students of color in two ways: Page Scholars get financial help for their post-secondary education, and in turn they spend at least fifty hours each year working with schoolchildren as real-life role models for success. Students at all levels of academic achievement can qualify to become a Page Scholar, which is awarded based on an applicant's educational goals, willingness to work with children, and financial need. Every student has potential, but many need support to realize their dreams.

Proceeds from the sale of this book help support the Page Education Foundation. To learn more about the Foundation and to order copies of the book, visit www.page-ed.org.

Photo by Håkan Carlsson

ALAN PAGE is an Associate Justice on the Minnesota Supreme Court. He was elected to the court in 1992 and reelected in 1998, 2004, and 2010. He is currently the Court's senior justice.

Alan was a defensive tackle with the Minnesota Vikings and the Chicago Bears from 1967 through 1981. He was selected as the NFL's Most Valuable Player in 1971 and elected to the Pro Football Hall of Fame in 1988.

Alan is an ardent defender of equal education for all children. He and his wife, Diane, are the founders of the Page Education Foundation, founded in 1988, which has awarded almost ten million dollars in scholarship grants. In 1981 Alan was named one of America's Ten Outstanding Young Men by the United States Jaycees, and in 1991 he received the National Education Association's Friend of Education award.

KAMIE PAGE is a second grade teacher who lives in Minneapolis, Minnesota. She doesn't have a perfectly pointy, impossibly perpendicular pinky, but she does love the way those words sound when they're said aloud. When she's not busy coming up with tricky tongue twisters, she's usually spending time with her husband, Ben, and their two bright and spunky children, Otis and Esther.

Kamie and Alan share a passion for children's literacy. Kamie's years in the classroom helping students develop a positive racial identity and Alan's years reading books to school children were the inspiration for this story. This is their second children's book.

Photo by Håkan Carlsson

Photo by Rebecca Felland-Syring

Minneapolis artist DAVID GEISTER has shared his passion for art and history with fellow enthusiasts, both young and old, in his paintings for various collectors, historical sites and museums, *The History Channel Magazine,* and several picture books, including *Alan and His Perfectly Pointy Impossibly Perpendicular Pinky, T Is for Twin Cities: A Minneapolis/St. Paul Alphabet, The Legend of Minnesota, Riding to Washington,* and *B Is for Battle Cry: A Civil War Alphabet,* written by his wife, author Patricia Bauer.

To teachers everywhere

—A. P.

To the "invisible you" in all of us and the
beauty to be found in our differences

—K. P.

To my dear family, who accept and love the "invisible me"

—D. G.

Page Education Foundation
P.O. Box 581254
Minneapolis, MN 55458
www.page-ed.org
info@page-ed.org

Printed and bound in the United States of America

First Edition

LCCN 2014918759

ISBN 978-0-692-31524-8

This book was expertly produced by Book Bridge Press.
www.bookbridgepress.com